Little Red
Robin

When the Tooth Fairy Forgot

Karen McCombie
Illusrated by Laura Hughes

SCHOLASTIC

For Maddie and Otis, and all their tiny, shiny teeth!

Scholastic Children's Books
An imprint of Scholastic Ltd.
Euston House, 24 Eversholt Street
London, NW1 1DB, UK
Registered office: Westfield Road, Southam, Warwickshire, CV47 0RA
SCHOLASTIC and associated logos are trademarks and/or registered
trademarks of Scholastic Inc.

First published in the UK in 2014 by Scholastic Ltd

Text copyright © Karen McCombie, 2014
Illustrations © Laura Hughes, 2014

The rights of Karen McCombie and Laura Hughes
to be identified as the author and illustrator of
this work have been asserted by them.

ISBN 978 1407 13897 8

A CIP catalogue record for this book is available from the British Library

Printed in China.

1 3 5 7 9 10 8 6 4 2

www.scholastic.co.uk

Chapter 1

"Good morning, Eddie!" says Eddie's teacher,
Miss Stevens.

Eddie sits on the carpet and says nothing.

"Good *morning*, Eddie!" Miss Stevens says again.

Miss Stevens is taking the register. She is calling
out the names of all the boys and girls in Eddie's
class.

Lots of them have said, "Good morning, Miss Stevens!" already.

Now everyone is waiting for Eddie to do the same. He doesn't.

"Eddie?" says Miss Stevens, glancing up from the register. "Is there a problem?"

Yes, but Eddie can't say so because of the wrong thing in his mouth.

Luckily, his best friend Nadia guesses what's happened.

"Please, miss!" Nadia says, waving her hand in the air. "I think Eddie's tooth has come out."

"Ah, I see," says Miss Stevens, passing him a tissue.

"Eddie was wiggling it when we were lining up
in the playground!" Nadia carries on.

"Thank you, Nadia." Miss Stevens smiles.
"Now, Eddie, just spit your tooth into the tissue,
and I'll take care of it until home time. You can
put it under your pillow for the Tooth Fairy tonight!"

4

Ooh, yes! I forgot about the Tooth Fairy, thinks Eddie, cheering up.

"Eddie was bending his tooth all the way forward and back," Nadia says. "It was really gross!"

Nadia likes gross stuff.
She likes examining snails.

She doesn't mind changing her little brother's
nappies.

And last week, when Polly fell off the
monkey bars and cut her knee,
everyone felt sick
except for Nadia.
She just went
"Whoo!" at all
the blood.

Eddie thinks his best friend might grow up to be a vet or a doctor.

Maybe she'll work in a hospital like the one his mum is going to have her baby in.

Eddie's baby sister will be born in about two weeks, his dad says.

That will be exciting.

But NOT as exciting as Eddie showing Mum and Dad his missing tooth!

Chapter 2

All day at school, Eddie has been practising his
Surprise Smile.

He's going to smile at Mum when she collects
him, and she will gasp when she sees the gap
where his tooth used to be.

But there is a problem.

Mum is *not* waiting in the playground.

Neither is Dad.

"Why is that weird girl waving at you?" asks Nadia.

The weird girl has pink, spiky hair, a pierced eyebrow and a T-shirt with a skull on.

"It's my big cousin Bella," Eddie tells Nadia.

Bella walks over to them.

"Hey, Eddie!" she says in a boomy voice.

"Hello," he says quietly.

Eddie isn't sure about Bella.

At family get-togethers, she is more interested in texting her teenage friends than talking to Eddie.

"So . . . guess what?" says Bella.

Nadia jumps in. "Is Eddie's mum having her baby right now?" she asks. (She is *very* good at guessing stuff.)

"Yes!" says Bella. "And Eddie's dad has asked me to babysit until they get back from the hospital."

Eddie feels a wobble in his tummy.

He wonders how long it takes to have a baby.

He hopes Mum can be back home in time to make his tea. . .

Chapter 3

Having a baby must take a *long* time.

It's now quarter-past bedtime, and Eddie's mum and dad STILL aren't back.

Bella has been looking after him, but she isn't very good at it.

She put on her
headphones as soon
as they got home.
(Mum and Eddie
always have an
after-school snuggle
on the sofa and
watch his favourite
TV programme
together.)

For tea she made
something in a
gloopy sauce that
smelled a bit burnt.

Then Eddie had to tell Bella when it was his bedtime.

And that she was meant to read him a story.

Eddie doesn't like today.

He didn't like having the tooth floating in his mouth this morning.

He didn't like Miss Stevens sounding cross when he didn't answer his name at register.

He didn't like spitting his tooth into a tissue (slobbery – yuck!).

He doesn't like Mum and Dad being at the hospital.

He doesn't like Bella babysitting him.

The only *good* thing about today is under his pillow.

Tonight, when Eddie is dreaming, the Tooth Fairy will come!

And in the morning, instead of a tiny white tooth, there'll be a shiny gold coin. . .

Chapter 4

The next day in the playground, Nadia comes
running up.

"Eddie, why are your eyes all red?" she asks.

She puts her arm around Eddie's shoulder. It feels so nice and friendly that he wants to cry. Again.

Eddie thinks he frightened Bella this morning when he cried.

Bella thought he must have hurt himself, but he was just really sad that there was nothing under his pillow except a stupid white tooth.

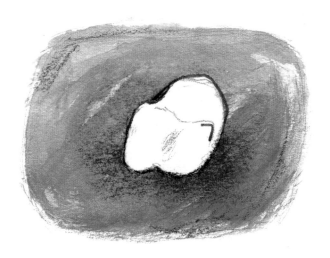

"The Tooth Fairy forgot to come. . ." he mumbles to Nadia, poking his tongue into the gap in his teeth.

Nadia stands straight up and slaps her hand across her mouth.

Everyone in class is shocked too, when Eddie tells them at circle time.

Even Miss Stevens tsk-tsk-tsks in a sorry-for-him sort of way.

But Eddie is *sure* things will be better by home time, because Mum or Dad will DEFINITELY be there.

Then Eddie can ask them *why* the Tooth Fairy forgot. . .

Chapter 5

When Eddie sees a flash of pink, spiky hair in the playground, he knows that his baby sister is being completely unfair. She is taking far too long to arrive.

"Wait until we get home, Eddie!" says Bella. "I have something AMAZING to show you."

"Is it the new baby?" asks Eddie.

"Nope," says Bella.

Eddie feels a thrill in his tummy as he follows his big cousin home.

"Go and look in your room, Eddie," says Bella, as soon as they get through the front door.

Eddie hurries to see what's happened.

Oh!

There is some kind of *trail* from the window to his bed. It's sparkly, silvery and fluttery.

"What is it?" Eddie asks, bending over to get a closer look at a wiggly line of sequins and ever-so-small squares of tissue.

"Well, I'm no expert," shrugs Bella, "but I think the twinkly stuff is fairy snot and that's *got* to be fairy-sized tissue!"

Eddie blinks.

Is Bella saying the *Tooth Fairy* left this behind?

"Eddie – what's that?"

He looks where Bella is pointing . . . and sees a tiny corner of paper peeking out from under his pillow.

Lifting the pillow, Eddie finds a note not much bigger than a stamp with tiddly writing on it. AND a shiny pound coin!

He grabs them both and scrunches his eyes to read what the note says.

Dear Eddie,

I'm sorry I couldn't come last night – I have had a really bad cold!

Love,

The Tooth Fairy xxx

"So, what do you think?" beams Bella.

"I think . . . I think it's pretty *whoo!*" says Eddie, copying his friend Nadia's favourite word.

Then before he knows it, Eddie is giving Bella a big, squeezy hug, and she's giving him one back!

Suddenly, they realize that they really like each other! They're so surprised that neither of them hears the key in the lock.

"HELLOOOOO!" a happy voice calls out. "ANYBODY WANT TO MEET A BRAND-NEW PERSON?"

Dad! With Mum! And Eddie's new baby sister!

He scrambles to his parents and there is a jumble of kisses and cuddles and chatting and Surprise Smiles. ("Oh, my! Where's your tooth gone, Eddie?" Mum exclaims.)

Eddie finds out that he is big brother to someone called Freya.

"So, what's been going on with *you*, Eddie?"
Dad asks, while Bella and Mum take turns
twiddling the baby's toes.

  With a smile, Eddie takes Dad by the hand and
leads him to his room.

"Look!" says Eddie, pointing to the silvery snot trail and the Tooth Fairy's sorry letter.

Dad nods and looks, oohs and aahs.

But then Eddie decides to say something that will *shock* Dad.

"Can I tell you a secret?" he whispers.

"Of course, Eddie," says Dad.

"It wasn't *really* the Tooth Fairy who did this. It was *Bella*!"

Dad's eyebrows ping right up to his hair.

"Really? How do you know that?" he asks Eddie.

"I saw a silver sequin glued to Bella's cheek," Eddie tells him. "I think she did all this to cheer me up because the REAL Tooth Fairy forgot."

"Yes, that makes sense!" Dad says, laughing. He laughs so hard he makes Eddie laugh too, even though he's not really sure what's so funny!

Chapter 6

The light is bright and the birds are tweeting ouside Eddie's window.

He is lying in his bed, feeling happier than happy, because Mum and Dad – and baby Freya – are back home and snoozing in the bedroom next door to his.

And Eddie is very happy now that he has TWO best friends: Nadia at school and his big cousin Bella.

Then Eddie thinks of something else . . . and quickly slides his hand under the pillow.

A coin!

The REAL Tooth Fairy had come in the night, just like he'd hoped she would.

Eddie doesn't know why she forgot the night Bella was looking after him. Maybe she had a cold after all – or toothache, maybe?

But it doesn't matter now.

"Thank you," he whispers to the Tooth Fairy.

He pictures a tiny winged thing fluttering away across the garden to her bed (wherever that is).

She is carrying his tooth.

She's sneezing tiny fairy sneezes. ("Atchoo. . . !")

And guess what?

She has pink, spiky hair. . .